To _Mommy_

Love _H S_

Hayden

First Candlewick Press hardcover edition 2003
First published in Great Britain in 1989 by Walker Books Ltd., London.

The Library of Congress has cataloged the paperback edition as follows:

Butterworth, Nick.
My mom is excellent / Nick Butterworth. — 1st U.S. ed.
Summary: A young boy describes all the amazing things that his mother can do.
ISBN 1-56402-289-7 (paperback)
[1. Mothers — Fiction.] I. Title.
PZ7.B98225Myj   1994
[E] — dc20   92-43769
ISBN 0-7636-2050-5 (hardcover)

2 4 6 8 10 9 7 5 3 1

Printed in Hong Kong

This book was typeset in New Century Schoolbook.
The illustrations were done in watercolor.

Candlewick Press
2067 Massachusetts Avenue
Cambridge, Massachusetts 02140

visit us at www.candlewick.com

MY MOM IS
EXCELLENT

Nick Butterworth

CANDLEWICK PRESS
CAMBRIDGE, MASSACHUSETTS

My mom is excellent.

She's a brilliant artist . . .

and she can balance
on a tightrope . . .

and she can fix anything . . .

and she tells the most
exciting stories . . .

and she's a fantastic gardener . . .

and she can swim like a fish . . .

and she can do amazing
tricks on a bike . . .

and she can knit anything . . .

and she can tame wild animals . . .

and she throws the best
parties in the world.

It's great to have
a mom like mine.

She's excellent!